HOW 7
WENT MAD

BY
BRAM STOKER

British Library Cataloguing-in-Publication Data
A catalogue record for this book is available from
the British Library

Bram Stoker

Abraham 'Bram' Stoker was born in Dublin, Ireland in 1847. Stoker was a semi-invalid as a child, and was bedridden until he started school at the age of seven. However, he made a full recovery and went on to excel as an athlete at Trinity College, which he enrolled at in 1864. Stoker graduated with honours in mathematics in 1870, and was also president of the university's philosophical society.

Stoker developed an interest in theatre, and became theatre critic for the *Dublin Evening Mail* in his early twenties. It was following a favourable review he gave of an 1876 Henry Irving production of *Hamlet* that Stoker and Irving struck up a friendship. Three years later, in the same year that Stoker married Florence Balcombe (whose former suitor was Oscar Wilde), he became acting-manager and then business manager of Irving's Lyceum Theatre – a post he went on to hold for 27 years. As a result of his close friendship with Irving (the most famous actor of his day), Stoker became something of a socialite. He mingled with London's high society, meeting writers such as Sir Arthur Conan Doyle, and travelled extensively in the United States, where he spent time with both Theodore Roosevelt and Walt Whitman.

While working for Irving, Stoker began to write novels, eventually producing a total of fifteen works of fiction. Although most met with at least mild success, Stoker is best known for his 1897 publication, *Dracula*. This work – an epistolary novel weaving hypnotism, magic, the supernatural, and other elements of Gothic fiction – went on to sell over one million copies, and has never been out of print. Today, the novel and its eponymous protagonist remain so well-known that one can actually visit the castle of Count Dracula in the Transylvanian region of Romania – despite the fact that Stoker never even went there himself.

After a series of strokes, Stoker died in London in 1912, aged 64.

HOW 7 WENT MAD.

N the bank of the river that flows through the Land there stands a beautiful palace, where one of the great men dwells.

The bank rises steep from the rushing water; and the great trees growing on the slope rise so high that their branches wave level with the palace turrets. It is a beautiful spot, where the grass is crisp and short and close like velvet, and as green as emerald. There the daisies shine like stars that have fallen, and lie scattered over the sward.

Many children have lived and grown to be men and women in the old palace, and they have had many pets. Amongst their pets have been many birds— for birds of all kinds love the place. In one corner is a spot which is called the Birds' Burying Ground. Here all the pets are laid when they die; and the grass grows greenly here, and many flowers spring up among the monuments.

Mr. Daw.

One of the boys that had here dwelt had once, as a pet, a raven. He found the bird, whose leg had been wounded, and took it home and nursed it till it grew well again; but the poor thing was lame.

Tineboy was the youth's name; and the bird was called Mr. Daw. As you may imagine, the raven loved the boy and never left him. There was a cage for it in his bedroom, and there the bird went every night to roost when the sun went down. Birds go to bed quite regularly of their own accord; and if you wished to punish a bird you would make him get up. Birds are not like boys and girls. Just fancy punishing boys or girls by not letting them go to bed at sunset, or by preventing them getting up very early in the morning.

Well, when morning came this bird would get up and stretch himself, and wink his eyes, and give a good shake all over, and then feel quite awake and ready to begin the day.

A bird has a much easier time of it in getting up than a boy or a girl. Soap cannot get into its eye; or the comb will not stick in knots of hair, and its shoe-laces never get into black knots. This is because it does not use soap, or combs, or shoe-laces; if it did, perhaps it also would suffer.

When Mr. Daw had quite finished his own dressing, he would hop on the bed and try and wake his master and make him get up; but of the two to wake him was the easier task. When the boy went to school the bird would fly along the road beside him, and would sit near

on a tree till school was over, and then would follow him home again in the same way.

Tineboy was very fond of Mr. Daw and he used sometimes to try to make him come into the schoolroom during school-hours. But the bird was very wise, and would not.

One day Tineboy was at his sums, and instead of attending to what he was doing, he kept trying to make Mr. Daw come in. The sum was " multiply 117,649 by 7." Tineboy and Mr. Daw kept looking at one another. Tineboy made signals to the bird to come in. Mr. Daw, however, would not stir; he sat outside in the shade, for the day was very hot, and put his head on one side and looked in knowingly.

" Come in, Mr. Daw," said Tineboy, " and help me to do this sum." Mr. Daw only croaked.

" Seven times nine are seventy-seven, seven times nine are seventy-nine—no ninety-seven. Oh, I don't know—I wish number 7 had never been invented," said Tineboy.

" Croak," said Mr. Daw.

The day was very hot and Tineboy was very sleepy. He thought that perhaps he would be able to do the sum better if he rested a little while, just to think; and so he put his head down on the table. He was not quite comfortable, for his forehead was on the 7, at least he thought it was; so he shifted it till it hung right down over the edge of the desk. Then, after a while, somehow, very queer things began to happen.

The Teacher was just going to tell them a story.

The scholars had all settled themselves down to listen ; the Raven sat on the sill of the open window, put his head on one side, closed one eye—the eye nearest the school-room—so that they might think him asleep, and listened away harder than any of them.

The pupils were all happy—all except three. One because his leg went to sleep ; another because she had her pocket full of curds and wanted to eat them, and

couldn't without being found out, and the curds were melting away ; and the third, who was awfully sleepy, and awfully anxious to hear the story, and couldn't do either because of the other.

The schoolmaster then began his story.

HOW POOR 7 WENT MAD.

"The Alphabet Doctor——"

Here he was interrupted by Tineboy, who said—

"*What is an Alphabet Doctor?*"

"An Alphabet Doctor," said the schoolmaster, "is the doctor who attends to the sicknesses and diseases of the letters of the Alphabet."

"*How have Alphabets diseases and sicknesses?*" asked Tineboy.

"Oh, they have plenty. Do you never make a crooked o or a capital A with a lame leg, or a T that is not straight in its back?"

There was a chorus from all the class, "He does. He does often." Ruffin, the biggest boy, said after all the others, "Very often. In fact always."

"Very well, then there must be some one to put them straight again, must there not?"

None of the children could say that there was not. Tineboy alone was heard to mutter to himself, "*I don't believe it.*"

The schoolmaster began again—

"The Alphabet Doctor was sitting down to his tea. He was very tired, for he had been out attending cases all day."

Tineboy again interrupted, " *What cases ?* "

" I can tell you. He had to put in an i which had been omitted, and to alter the leg of an R which had been twisted into a **B**.

" Well, just as he was beginning his tea a hurried knock came to the door. He went to the door, opened it, and a groom rushed into the room, breathless with running, and said—

"' Oh, Doctor, do come quick ; there is a frightful calamity down at our place.'

" ' What is our place ? ' said the doctor.

" ' Oh, you know. The Number Stables.' "

" *What are the Number Stables ?* " said Tineboy, again interrupting.

" The Number Stables," said the Teacher, " are the stables where the numbers are kept."

" *Why are they kept in stables ?* " said Tineboy.

" Because they go so fast."

" *How do they go fast ?* "

" You take a sum and work it and you will see at once. Or look at your multiplication table ; it starts with twice one are two, and before you get down the page you are at twelve times twelve. Is that not fast going ?

" Well, they have to keep the numbers in stables, or else they would run away altogether and never be heard of again. At the end of the day they all come home and

change their shoes, and get tied up and have their
supper.

" The Groom from the Number Stables was very
impatient.

" ' What is wrong ? ' said the Doctor.

" ' Oh, poor 7, sir.'

" ' What of him ? '

" ' He is mortal bad.   We don't think he'll ever get
through it.'

" ' Through what ? ' said the Doctor.

" ' Come and see,' said the Groom.

" The Doctor hurried away, taking the lantern with
him, for the night was dark, and soon got to the
Stables.

" As he got close there was a very curious sound
heard—a sound of gasping and choking, and yelling
and coughing, and laughing, and a wild, unearthly
screech all in one.

" ' Oh, do come quick ! ' said the Groom.

" When the Doctor entered the stables there was poor
No. 7 with all the neighbours round him, and he was
in a very bad way.   He was foaming at the mouth and
apparently quite mad.   The Nurse from the Grammar
Village was holding him by the hand, trying to bleed
him.   All the neighbours were wringing either their hands
or their necks, or were helping to hold him.   The Footsmith,—the man," explained the teacher, seeing from the

look on Tineboy's face that he was going to ask a question,
" the man who puts the feet on the letters and numbers
to make them able to stand upright without wearing out,
—was holding down the poor demented number.

" The Nurse, trying to quiet him, said :

" ' There now, there now, deary—don't go and make
a noise. Here comes the good Alphabet Doctor, who
will make you unmad.'

" ' I won't be made unmad,' said 7, loudly.

" ' But, my good sir,' said the Doctor, 'this cannot go
on. You surely are not mad enough to insist on being
mad ? '

" ' Yes, I am,' said 7, loudly.

" ' Then,' said the Doctor blandly, 'if you are mad
enough to insist on being mad, we must try to cure your
madness or being mad, and then you will be unmad
enough to wish to be unmad, and we will cure that
too.' "

" *I don't understand that,*" said Tineboy.

" Hush ! " said the class.

" The Doctor took out his stethoscope, and his telescope, and his microscope, and his horoscope, and began
to use them on poor mad 7.

" First he put the stethoscope to the sole of his foot,
and began to talk into it.

" ' That is not the way to use that,' said the Nurse ;
' you ought to put it to his chest and listen to it.'

The Interrogation.

"'Not at all, my dear madam,' said the bland Doctor, 'that is the way with sane people; but, of course, when one is insane, the fact of the disease necessitates an opposite method of treatment.' Then he took the telescope and looked at him to see how near he was, and the microscope to look how small; and then he drew his horoscope."

" *Why did he draw it ?* " said Tineboy.

" Because, my dear child," said the Teacher, " do you not see that by right a horoscope is cast; but as the poor man was mad the horoscope had to be drawn."

" *What is a horrorscope ?*" said Tineboy.

" It is not horrorscope, my child; it is horoscope—a very different thing."

" *Well, what is horoscope ?* "

" Look in your dictionary, my dear child," said the Teacher.

" Well, when the doctor had used all the instruments, he said, ' I use all these in order to find the scope of the disease. I shall now proceed to find the cause. In the first instance, I shall interrogate the patient.'

"' Now, my good sir, why do you insist on being mad ? '

"' Because I choose.'

"' Oh, my dear sir, that is not a polite answer. Why do you choose ? '

"' I can't say why,' said 7, ' unless I make a speech.'

" ' Well, make a speech.'

" ' I can't speak till I am set free; how can I make a speech with all these people holding me?'

" ' We are afraid to let you go,' said the Nurse, ' you will run away.'

" ' I will not.'

" ' You promise that?' said the doctor.

" ' I promise,' said 7.

" ' Let him go,' said the Doctor, and accordingly they put a piece of carpet under him, and the Footsmith sat on his head, the way they do when horses fall down in the street. Then they all got clear away, and the Footsmith got away too; and after a long struggle 7 got to his feet.

" ' Now make the speech,' said the Doctor.

" ' I can't begin,' said 7, ' till I get a glass of water on a table. Who ever heard of any one making a speech without a glass of water!'

" So they brought a glass of water.

" ' Ladies and Gentlemen—' began 7, and then stopped.

" ' What are you waiting for?' said the Doctor.

" ' For the applause, of course,' said 7. ' Who ever heard of a speech without applause?'

" They all applauded.

" ' I am mad,' said 7, ' because I choose to be mad; and I never shall, will, might, could, should, would, or ought to be anything but mad. The treatment that I get is enough to make me mad.'

" ' Dear me, dear me !' said the Doctor. ' What treatment ?'

" ' Morning, noon, and night am I treated worse than any slave. There is not in the whole range of learning any one thing that has so much to bear as I have. I work hard all the time. I never grumble. I am often a multiple ; often a multiplicand. I am willing to bear my share of being a result, but I cannot stand the treatment I get. I am wrong added, wrong divided, wrong subtracted, and wrong multiplied. Other numbers are not treated as I am ; and, besides, they are not orphans like me.'

" ' Orphans ? ' asked the Doctor ; 'what do you mean ?'

" ' I mean that the other numbers have lots of relations. But I have neither kith nor kin -except old Number 1, and he does not count for much ; and, besides, I am only his great-great-great-great-grandson.'

" ' How do you mean ? ' asked the Doctor.

" ' Oh, he is an old chap that is there all the time. He has all his children round him, and I only come six generations down.'

" ' Humph !' said the doctor.

" ' Number 2,' went on 7, 'never gets into any trouble, and 4, 6, and 8 are his cousins. Number 3 is close to 6 and 9. No. 5 is half a decimal and he never gets into trouble. But as for me, I am miserable, ill-.

treated, and alone.' Here poor 7 began to cry, and bending down his head sobbed bitterly."

When the Teacher got thus far there was an interruption, for here little Tineboy began to cry too.

" Why are you crying?" said Ruffin, the bully boy.

"*I am not crying*," said Tineboy, and he cried away faster than ever.

The Teacher went on with the story.

" The Alphabet Doctor tried to cheer poor 7.

"' Hear, hear !' said he.

"7 stopped crying and looked at him. ' No,' said he, ' you should say " speak, speak," it is I that should say " hear, hear." '

" ' Certainly,' said the Doctor, ' you would say that if you were sane; but then, you see, you are not sane, and being mad you say what you should not say.'

" ' That is false,' said 7.

"' I understand,' said the Doctor, ' but do not stop to argue the point. If you were sane you would say " that is true," but you do say " that is false," meaning that you agree with me.'

" 7 looked pleased at being so understood.

" ' No,' said he—meaning ' yes.'

"' Then,' continued the Doctor, 'if you say " speak, speak," when a sane man would say " hear, hear," of course, I should say "hear, hear," when I mean "speak, speak," because I am talking to a madman.'

"'No, no,' said 7—meaning, 'yes, yes.'

"'Go on with your speech,' said the Doctor.

"No 7 took out his handkerchief and wept.

"'Ladies and Gentlemen,' he went on, 'once more I must plead the cause of the poor ill-used number—that is me—this orphan number—this number without kin ——'"

Here Tineboy interrupted the Teacher, "*How had he no skin?*"

"Kin, my child. Kin, not skin," said the Teacher.

"*What is the difference between kin and skin?*" asked Tineboy.

"There will be but a small difference," said the Teacher, "between this cane and your skin if you interrupt." So Tineboy was quiet.

"Well," said the teacher, "poor 7 went on—'I implore your pity for this forlorn number. Oh, you boys and girls, think of a poor desolate number, who has no home, no friends, no father, mother, brother, sister, uncle, aunt, nephew, niece, son, daughter, or cousin, and is desolate and alone.'"

Tineboy here set up a terrible howl.

"What are you crying for?" said the Teacher.

"*I want poor old 7 to be more happy. I will give him some of my lunch and a share of my bed.*"

The Teacher turned to the Monitor.

" Tineboy is a good child," he said, " let him for the next week learn 7 times o up, and perhaps that will comfort him."

The Raven, sitting in the window, winked his eye to himself and hopped about with a suppressed merry croak, shook his wings, and seemed hugging himself and laughing. Then he hopped softly away, and stole up and hid on the top of the book-case.

The Schoolmaster went on with his story.

" Well, children, after a while poor 7 got better and promised that he would get unmad. Before the Doctor went home again all the Alphabet and Number Children came and shook poor Number 7's hand, and promised that they would be more kind to him in future.

" Now, children, what do you think of the story ? "

They all said that they liked it, that it was beautiful, and that they too would try to be more kind to poor 7 for the future. At last Ruffin the bully boy said :

" I don't believe it. And if it is true I wish he had died ; we would be better without him."

" Would we?" asked the teacher, " how ? "

" Because we would not be troubled with him," said Ruffin.

As he said it there was a sort of queer croak heard from the Raven, but nobody minded, except Tineboy, who said :—

Mr. Daw's Task.

" Mr. Daw, you and I love poor 7, at all events."

The Raven hated Ruffin because he always threw stones at him, and he had tried to pull the feathers out of his tail, and when Ruffin spoke, his croak seemed to mean, " Just you wait." When no one was looking Mr. Daw stole up and hid in the rafters.

Then presently school broke up, and Tineboy went home ; but he was not able to find Mr. Daw. He thought he was lost, and was very miserable, and went to bed crying.

In the meantime, when the school was locked up empty, Mr. Daw came down from the rafters very, very quietly—hobbled over to the door, and putting his head down, listened ; then he flew and scrambled up on the handle of the door, and looked out through the keyhole. There was nothing to see and nothing to hear.

Then he got up on the Master's desk, flapped his wings, and began to crow like a cock, only very softly, for fear he should be heard.

Presently he went over all the room, flying up to the big sheets of multiplication table, and turning over the pages of the books with his claws, and picking up SOME-THING with his sharp beak.

One would hardly believe it, but he was stealing all the Number Sevens in the place ; he picked the Seven off the clock, rubbed it off the slates, and brushed it with his wings off the blackboard.

Mr. Daw knew that if once you can get the whole

of any number out of a schoolroom no one else can use it without asking your leave.

Whilst he was picking out all the Sevens he was swelling out very much ; and when he had got them all he was exactly Seven times his natural size.

He was not able to do this all at once. It took him the whole night, and when he got back to his corner in the rafters it was nearly time for school to open.

He was now so big that he was only just able to squeeze into the corner and no more.

The school time came, but there was no Master, and there were no Scholars. A whole hour passed; and then the Master came, and the Ushers, and all the Boys and Girls.

When they were all in the Master said—

" You are all very late."

" Please, sir, we could not help it," they all answered together.

" Why could you not help it ? "

They all answered at once—

" I wasn't called in time."

" What time are you called at every morning ? "

They all seemed about to speak, but all were silent.

" Why don't you answer ? " asked the Teacher.

They made motions with their mouths like speaking, but no one said anything.

The Raven up in his corner croaked a quiet laugh all to himself.

A Lost Hour.

" Why don't you answer ? " asked the Teacher again. " If I have not my question answered at once, I shall keep you all in."

" Please, sir, we can't," said one.

" Why not ? "

" Because "—

Here Tineboy interrupted, " *Why were you so late, sir?*"

" Well, my boy, I am sorry to say I was late; but the fact is, my servant did not knock at my door at the usual hour."

" *What hour, sir ?*" asked Tineboy.

The Teacher seemed as if he was going to speak, but stopped.

" This is very queer," he said, after a long pause.

Ruffin said, in a sort of swaggering way, " We are not late at all.   You are here and we are here—that is all."

" No, it is not all," said the Teacher.   " Ten is the hour, and it is now eleven—we have lost an hour."

" How have we lost it ? " asked one of the Scholars.

" Well, that is what puzzles me.   We must only wait a little and see."

Here Tineboy said suddenly, " *Perhaps some one stole it !*"

" Stole what ? " said the scholars.

" *I don't know*," said Tineboy.

They all laughed.

" *You need not laugh, something is stolen; look at my*

lesson !" said Tineboy, and he held up the book. Here is what they saw—

—	1	are	—
—	2	,,	14
—	3	,,	21
—	4	,,	28
—	5	,,	35
—	6	,,	42
—	—	,,	49
—	8	,,	56
—	9	,,	63
—	10	,,	—o

All the Scholars crowded round Tineboy to look at the book. Ruffin did not, for he was looking at the school clock.

" The clock has lost something," said he, and sure enough it did not look all right.

The Teacher looked up—for he was leaning with his head on his desk, groaning.

" What is wrong with it ? " he asked.

"Something is missing."

" There · is a number out ; there are only eleven figures," said the Teacher.

" No, no," said the Scholars.

" Count them out, Ruffin," said the Master.

" 1 2 3 4 5 6 8 9 10 11 12."

" Quite right," said the Teacher, " you see there are twelve. No there are not—yes there are—no—yes—no, yes—what is it all about?" and he looked round the room, and then leaned his head on the desk again and groaned.

In the meantime the Raven had crept along the rafters till he had got over the Teacher's desk; and then he got a good heavy Seven and dropped it right on the little bald spot on the top of the Teacher's head. It bounded off the head and fell on the desk before him. The instant the Teacher saw it he knew what was wanting all the time. He covered over the Seven with a piece of blotting paper. He then called up Ruffin.

"Ruffin, you told me that something was missing—are you sure?"

"Yes, of course."

"Very well. Do you remember that you said yesterday, that you wished a certain Number had died in a madhouse?"

"Yes, I do; and I wish it still."

"Well, that Number has been stolen by some one during the night."

"Hurrah!" said Ruffin, and he threw his book up to the ceiling. It hit poor Mr. Daw, who had another Seven in his beak ready to drop it, and knocked the Seven down. It fell into Tineboy's cap, which he held in his hand. He took it out, and stooped and petted it.

"*Poor 7,*" said Tineboy.

"Give me the Number," said Ruffin.

"*I shan't. It belongs to me.*"

"Then I'll make you," said Ruffin; and he caught hold of Tineboy—even before the Master's face.

"*Let me go. I'll not give you my poor Seven,*" said Tineboy, and he began to scream and cry.

"Ruffin, stand out," said the Master.

Ruffin did so.

"Seven times seven?" asked the Master.

Ruffin did not answer. He could not, for he had not got a Seven.

"*I know,*" said Tineboy.

"Oh, yes," said Ruffin, with a sneer; "he knows because he has a Number."

"*Forty-nine,*" said Tineboy.

"Right," said the Master; "go up, Tineboy."

So Tineboy went up to the top of the class, and Ruffin went down.

"Seven times forty-nine?" asked the Master.

They were all silent.

"Come, answer!" said the Master.

"*What is it, yourself?*" said Tineboy.

"Well, my boy, I am sorry to say I cannot say. Dear me, it is very queer," and the Master put down his head on the desk again, and groaned louder than ever.

Just then Mr. Daw took another seven and dropped it down on the floor before Tineboy.

"Three hundred and forty-three," said Tineboy, quickly; for he could answer as he had another Seven.

The Teacher looked up and laughed loudly.

" Hurrah, hurrah ! " said he.

When the third Seven fell the Raven began to swell.

He got seven times as big as he was, so that he began to lift the slates off the roof.

The Scholars all looked up ; Ruffin had his mouth open, and Mr. Daw, anxious to get rid of the Sevens, dropped one into it.

" Two thousand three hundred and one," Ruffin spluttered out.

Mr. Daw dropped another Seven into his mouth, and he spluttered out again worse than ever, " Sixteen thousand eight hundred and seven."

The Raven began hurling Sevens at him as fast as he could ; and each time he threw one he grew smaller and smaller, till he got to just his natural size.

Ruffin kept spluttering out and gasping numbers as hard as ever he could, till he grew black in the face and fell down in a fit just as he had come to " Seventy-nine thousand seven hundred and ninety-two billion, two hundred and sixty-six thousand two hundred and ninety-seven million six hundred and twelve thousand and one."

Suddenly Tineboy woke up, and found that he had been dreaming with his head down.

www.ingramcontent.com/pod-product-compliance
Lightning Source LLC
Chambersburg PA
CBHW030544180626
46810CB00005B/2004